Is This Guy for Real?

Bus Five pulled over and the doors opened wide. Natalie and James took one look inside—and jumped back in surprise. The new bus driver was wearing a polka-dot shirt, checkered high-top sneakers, and a hat with cloth moose antlers.

"*Bonjour*. I am Rick DeVries, zee new host for Bus Five," he said in a fake French accent. "Please to come in and sit down."

Natalie didn't budge. Rick DeVries looked like a clown and he talked like a cartoon character. There was no telling what might happen with him behind the wheel.

The Kids on Bus Five

#1 The Bad News Bully

#2 Wild Man at the Wheel

Available from MINSTREL Books

THE KIDS ON BUS FIVE

WILD MAN AT THE WHEEL

BY MARCIA LEONARD

Illustrated
by Julie Durrell

A MINSTREL® BOOK

Published by POCKET BOOKS
New York   London   Toronto   Sydney   Tokyo   Singapore

For Hannah Michel, Anna Carroll,
and Julianna Carlson—
the real Hannah, Anna, and Janna.
—M. L.
For all the folks at the Vocell Bus Company.
—J.D.

A MINSTREL PAPERBACK *Original*

 A Minstrel Book published by
POCKET BOOKS, a division of Simon & Schuster Inc.
1230 Avenue of the Americas, New York, NY 10020

Copyright © 1996 by Small Packages, Inc.

ISBN: 0-671-54191-9

First Minstrel Books printing September 1996

10 9 8 7 6 5 4 3 2 1

A MINSTREL BOOK and colophon are registered trademarks of Simon & Schuster Inc.

Cover art by Julie Durrell

Printed in the U.S.A.

Chapter One

Old Yeller

Natalie Adams glanced at the kitchen clock. "Quarter to eight. Time to go," she said to her best friend, James Penny. "We don't want to be late and give Mr. Balter a reason to yell at us."

"Old Yeller doesn't need a reason," James retorted. "He shouts no matter what we do."

"True." Natalie sighed. "I sure wish we had a different bus driver."

"Me, too," said James. "This is our fourth year with Mr. Balter—and that's four too many." He brushed some crumbs from his Save the Wolves shirt. Then he cleared his place. "Okay, Nat. I'm ready," he said.

It was Monday morning. James's mom had dropped him off at the Adamses' house on her way to work. She'd done that every school day since he and Nat were in kindergarten. They always ate breakfast together. Then they rode the bus together to Maple Street School.

Natalie picked up her backpack and lunch box. Then she called her younger brother. "Cody! Where are you? Come on, or we'll be late for the bus."

"I'm up here in my room," Cody called back. "I'll be down in a minute."

Nat rolled her eyes. "If you don't come now, we're leaving without you."

Mrs. Adams came downstairs. "Be patient, Nat," she said. "You and James are big third graders. Cody's only in kindergarten. You can wait a few minutes for him."

Just then Cody came racing down the stairs. "Here I am," he said. "I just had to get these." He held up a stack of superhero

trading cards. "Which would you rather be, James—Swamp Thing or Trash Master?"

"Hmmm," said James. "Would I rather be a slimy green lizard man or a creature made of garbage?" He shook his head. "Gee, Cody. That's a tough one. I can't decide."

"Because they're both so cool?" said Cody.

"Because they're both so gross," said Nat.

She and Cody gave their mom a hug. Then the three kids hurried to the school bus stop at the end of the drive.

Natalie gazed down the road, shading her eyes against the early morning sun. She could see the school bus rounding the bend.

"Here comes bad old Bus Five," she said to James. "Are you ready for our game? How many times will he say it today?"

"I guess...five times," said James.

"I guess six," said Nat. "That's how many times he said it on Friday, remember?"

Cody looked up from his trading cards. "Said what? Who are you guys talking about?"

"Mr. Balter," Natalie said. "We're trying to guess how many times he'll say 'sit down' before we get to school."

"You mean, how many times he'll yell it," James said.

"Let me play. Let me play." Cody hopped up and down. "I guess two times."

Natalie tossed back her thick blond braid. "That's way too low," she scoffed.

Cody crossed his arms. "It is not."

"Oh, all right. Have it your way," Nat replied. The bus stopped at the drive, and she and James got on board. Cody followed. He was a little slow climbing the steep steps, and Mr. Balter got impatient.

"Hurry up! Hurry up!" yelled Mr. Balter.

Cody tried to hurry. He tripped on the top step. Luckily, he caught himself before he fell. But the trading cards flew out of his hands and landed all over the floor.

"My cards!" Cody cried. He scrambled to pick them up. Nat and James helped.

Mr. Balter scowled at them. "When will you kids learn to leave your junk at home?" he bellowed. "Now take a seat, all of you."

"What a grouch," Cody muttered as they walked down the aisle. Then he grinned. "Hey, Nat," he said loudly. "Mr. Balter said, 'take a seat.' Does that count? It's almost the same as 'sit down.'"

"No, it doesn't count—and keep your voice down, Cody," Nat whispered back. "I don't want Old Yeller to know about our game. He's grumpy enough as it is."

James and Cody took a seat together. Natalie sat behind them. She slipped off her backpack and smoothed down her new shirt. It was white with colorful cowboy boots printed across the front. One pair even matched the red cowboy boots she always wore.

Celia Cruz leaned across the aisle. "Hi, Nat," she said. "I really like your shirt."

"Thanks!" said Natalie. She flushed with

pleasure. Celia was a fifth grader and the most popular girl at Maple Street School. A compliment from her was extra nice.

It's funny, thought Nat. *A few weeks ago, Celia would have been sitting in the back of the bus, talking with her friends. She never would have noticed me or my new shirt. But now everything's different—and it's all because of Hank Martin.*

Natalie leaned forward to talk to James and Cody. "You know what?" she said. "I think Hank did Bus Five a favor."

"Hank the Tank?" Cody squeaked.

"That bully never did anything nice in his whole life," James said.

"I don't mean on purpose," Nat said. "But remember how kids on this bus used to sit in the same seats every day? Remember how they talked to their friends and nobody else?"

"Yeah," James said slowly. "So?"

"So, after we all teamed up to stop Hank

7

from picking on us, everything changed," Nat said. "Now everyone's a lot friendlier, and we sit in different places all the time." She flung out an arm. "See what I mean?"

The three of them looked around. Celia was sitting with Kate Ziegler, who was in Nat and James's third-grade class. A fourth grader named Jamal Dixon was talking about karate with a second grader named Dylan Mahoney. And a first grader was telling knock-knock jokes to some kindergartners.

James turned to Nat in surprise. "Maybe you're right. Maybe Hank *did* do us a favor. Bus Five is pretty nice these days."

"Except for Old Yeller," Cody grumbled.

Natalie nodded. "Except for him."

A few minutes later, the bus stopped and Cody's friend Eli Hirsch got on. "Eli!" Cody called. "Want to see my superhero cards?"

"Sure," said Eli. He paused by Cody's seat to take a look.

"Sit down! Sit down!" Mr. Balter yelled.

"That's two times," Cody said gleefully.

Eli took a seat across the aisle. "What's two times?" he asked.

"Forget it, Eli. Cody has a big mouth." Natalie frowned at her brother.

"Okay, okay. I get the message," Cody said. He passed some cards to his friend. "Here, Eli. Check these out."

Eli went through the cards one by one. "Wow! You've got Captain Courage. She's really great."

"I've got Sergeant Strong Arm, too," said Cody. "Wait. I'll find him for you." He fished through his stack for the card.

The bus stopped and Hank Martin got on. Cody didn't look up, but Natalie did. Hank the Tank was bigger than the other fifth graders—and stronger, too. He'd promised not to pick on kids anymore. But Nat still didn't trust him. She watched him closely as he started down the aisle.

Cody found the card he wanted. Without

looking, he leaned over to hand it to Eli—
and bumped right smack into Hank.

"Ooof!" said Cody. Then he saw who it
was, and his eyes widened with fear. The
card dropped from his fingers. "Sorry,
Hank," he said in a small voice.

"It was an accident," James said quickly.

"Cody didn't mean to bump you," Natalie
added. She tensed, waiting to see what
Hank would do. If he tried anything with
her brother...

But Hank just picked up the card. "Huh,"
he grunted. "Sergeant Strong Arm. You like
him?"

Cody nodded, his eyes still wide.

"Me, too. I think he's cool," said Hank.
He handed Cody the card. Then he stomped
to the back of the bus and sat down by
himself.

Natalie looked at James in wonder. "Did
you see that, or was I dreaming?"

"I saw it," James said. "But I don't believe

it. Hank actually gave back the card. He didn't rip it up or anything."

"Maybe he likes superheroes," said Nat.

"Maybe he's changed," said Cody.

"I guess it's possible," James said slowly. "People do change sometimes."

Just then two kindergarten kids started singing, "The wheels on the bus go round and round, round and round, round and round...."

"Stop that racket!" shouted Mr. Balter. "You're giving me a headache to go with my stomachache."

Natalie sighed. "Maybe *some* people change. But not Old Yeller."

Chapter Two

A Wish Comes True

By the time Bus Five reached Maple Street School, Mr. Balter had yelled lots of times. But he'd said "sit down" only twice.

The kids filed off the bus. "What's with Old Yeller?" Natalie asked James. "He usually gets to five 'sit down's at least."

"Who knows," said James. "Maybe he really does have a headache and a stomachache."

"You guys are just bad losers," said Cody. "I guessed two and I was right—thanks to my lucky T-shirt."

"That ratty old thing? I thought Mom put it in the ragbag," Natalie said.

"No way," said Cody. He lifted his red turtleneck. Underneath was a worn T-shirt with a picture of a monster on the front.

"Gross," said Nat. "Cover it up, Cody." She tried to grab him, but he dodged away. Then the bell rang, and they all went inside.

Nat and James hurried to class. Their teacher, Ms. Donovan, was waiting by the door. She had short spiky hair and little round glasses. Today she was wearing a long floaty skirt and a blue jean vest.

"Hi, kids! Come on in," she said. "I have some news to share with you. Then we'll get started with our regular day."

Natalie and James grinned. There was no such thing as a regular day in Ms. Donovan's class. She liked to surprise her students.

When everyone was seated, Ms. Donovan held up a sheet of paper. "I have an announcement about the Fall Fun Fair," she said. "The PTA would like some new games and activities for this year's fair. They're asking each class for one idea—by next Monday."

She smiled at the kids. "So what do you think? Can we come up with something really great by then?"

"Yes!" everyone said.

Right away, Warren Smiley raised his hand.

"Save that idea, Warren," said Ms. Donovan. "The rest of you do some thinking, too. We'll talk about this again on Friday." She put the note on her desk. "Right now it's time for writing practice."

"The curse of cursive," Nat muttered.

"Come on, Natalie. This will be fun," said her teacher. "Think for a minute. What do you want to do when you grow up?"

Natalie didn't need a minute. "I want to live in Montana and raise horses and ride them all the time," she said in a rush.

"Okay," said Ms. Donovan. "Imagine that you're famous—the star of the rodeo—and someone asks for your autograph. Are you going to print your name? Or are you going to write it in beautiful, flowing cursive?"

Nat sighed. "Cursive, I guess."

"Good," said Ms. Donovan. She turned to the other kids. "That's what each of you will be working on this morning. Your signature—the special way you write your name. So from now on, whenever you turn in homework, you can autograph it for me."

Natalie had to smile. As usual, Ms. Donovan made the hard stuff fun. But all the same, Nat was glad that "Natalie Adams" didn't have lots of letters.

Ms. Donovan passed out sheets of lined paper. Nat's name was written in cursive at the top of hers. Slowly she copied the letters. *N-a-t-a-l-i-e*. She tried to make them flow together. But they didn't really look like the example. Still, she kept on trying, and while she practiced, she thought about the Fall Fun Fair.

She and James and their families had been going to the fair for years. It was held on a Saturday in the middle of October, and there were always lots of games, plenty of arts and crafts, and loads of food.

What could we do that would be different? Nat wondered.

By the end of the practice session, her signature had improved a little. But she didn't have any great ideas for the fair.

Later, at lunchtime, she and James talked it over with Kate and Warren.

"What's the idea you had this morning?" James asked Warren.

"I want to do something really gross and messy," Warren said. "A pie-eating contest. Or mud wrestling."

"Yuck!" said Kate. "How about a treasure hunt? Or maybe we could put on a play."

Just then Hannah, Anna, and Janna raced over to the table. They were second graders, and they also rode Bus Five.

"Hi, you guys," said Hannah.

"We just found out something really interesting," said Anna.

"It's about Mr. Balter," said Janna.

James grinned. "Let me guess. He won first prize in a grumpy bus driver contest?"

"Wrong," said Janna. "Guess again."

"He lost his voice from yelling so much— and now he can't find it," Warren said.

"You're almost right," said Anna.

"Mr. Balter's got the flu. He went home sick," said Hannah.

"Are you sure?" asked Nat. "Mr. Balter's never sick. He hasn't missed one single day since I've been riding Bus Five."

"I'm sure," said Janna. "I took some papers to the principal's office, and I heard her talking about it. A substitute driver took the morning kindergartners home."

James poked Natalie. "Hey, you got your wish! Remember this morning you wished for a different driver? Well, now we have one."

"Too bad you didn't wish for a hundred bucks, too," said Warren.

Natalie laughed. "That's okay. I'll settle for a new driver."

"I wonder what he'll be like," said James.

"Or she," put in Kate.

"Who cares," Nat said. "Anyone will be better than Mr. Balter, right?"

"Right!" everyone said together.

James and Natalie were a little late leaving class at the end of the school day. So when they got to Bus Five, there was already a crowd of kids waiting to board.

James craned his neck, trying to peer around some tall fifth graders. "Can you see our new driver?" he asked Natalie.

"No, but I can sure hear her," Nat said.

The driver was loudly greeting each kid who got on the bus. "Hi, I'm Maybelle Malinowski. Call me May—everyone does. Hi, glad to meet you. I'm filling in while Mr. Balter's sick."

"Man, she's almost as loud as Old Yeller," said James.

"Yeah, but she sounds a whole lot nicer," said Nat. "She's actually talking to kids. Old Yeller never did that."

The line inched forward. Finally, Nat and James were close enough to get a good look at May. She had a round face, curly brown hair, and a big, friendly smile.

"Hi, there," she said as Nat and James got on the bus. "How was school today?"

"Fine," Nat said, smiling back.

"Good. Glad to hear it," said May. "Do you have lots of homework?"

"Not too much," said James.

"Do it right away when you get home," said May. "Work first, then play. That's what I always say."

She gave them a wink. Then she turned to greet the last few kids in line. "Hi! It's great to see so many smiling faces. Uh-oh, better tie that shoe. If you ask me, that's an accident waiting to happen."

James and Nat slipped into an empty seat. He nudged her with his elbow. "So what do you think of May?"

"I like her," said Natalie.

"Me, too," said James. "She's friendly—unlike Old Yeller."

Natalie looked at the toes of her cowboy boots. "This is going to sound mean," she said slowly. "But I kind of hope Mr. Balter stays sick for a while."

James nodded. "Then we could keep May for our driver."

"Yeah." Nat sighed. "But I bet it won't happen. I bet Mr. Balter's back tomorrow, as mean as ever."

Chapter Three

Mother-May-I

The next morning Natalie, James, and Cody were ready for school early. They couldn't wait to see who was driving Bus Five.

"Come on!" Cody said to the others. "Last one to the bus stop is a rotten egg." He grabbed his backpack by one strap. Then he raced out the door and down the drive. He didn't notice that his pack was open.

"Cody, stop! You're losing all your stuff!" Natalie yelled. She followed behind him, picking up pencils and markers, a bunch of seashells, three minicars, two superhero action figures, and a library book.

Cody picked up things from his end of the drive. He was reaching for some loose papers when a sudden breeze sent them flying.

"Hey! My papers!" he shouted.

"Don't worry, I'll get them," called James. He chased after the papers, dashing back and forth across the lawn until he caught them. Then he brought them to Cody.

Natalie came over, too. Her arms were full of Cody's stuff. "Here, I think this is everything," she said.

"Thanks, you guys," Cody said. "I'll just check to make sure nothing's missing."

Nat rolled her eyes. "How could you tell, with all this junk?"

"It's not junk," Cody snapped. "It's important stuff." He put the heavier things back in the bottom of his pack. Then he shuffled through the papers. "Oh, no!" he wailed. "My Sergeant Strong Arm stickers! They must've blown away."

He began to search the yard.

Just then Bus Five pulled up to the stop—with Maybelle Malinowski behind the wheel.

Nat punched the air with her fist. "All right, it's May! Mr. Balter must still be sick. Let's go. Forget the stickers, Cody."

"No way," said Cody. "I need them."

James and Nat headed for the bus. "Come on, Cody," called James. "We'll find the stickers later, I promise."

Cody ignored him and kept looking.

Natalie was just about to go back to drag her brother from the yard, when suddenly he reached under a bush.

"Here they are!" he shouted happily. He ran to the bus, waving the stickers. Then he climbed on board behind Nat and James.

"Hi, kids," May said in a cheery voice. She glanced at a list taped to the dashboard. "Let's see. Natalie, James, and Cody—right?"

"Right," they all said.

"Good. I like to know my riders," said

24

May. She turned to Cody. "From now on, young man, please be ready and waiting at the bus stop. The early boy catches the school bus, I always say." She gave him a wink.

"Yes, May," Cody said meekly. He took a seat with Jamal. Nat and James sat behind them, across from Celia.

"Boy, May sure is different from Mr. Balter," James said. "He would have yelled at Cody for holding up the bus. But she was really nice about it."

"She wanted to know our names, too," said Nat. "Old Yeller couldn't care less who we are." She heaved a big sigh. "Too bad May doesn't drive Bus Five all the time."

"She used to," Celia put in. "I think she just substitutes now. But I had her for two years before Mr. Balter took over."

"Lucky you," said Natalie. "It must have been great having a friendly driver instead of a crabby one."

Jamal turned in his seat. "There's such a thing as too friendly," he said frowning.

"What do you mean?" asked James.

"Just wait. You'll find out soon enough," said Jamal.

Celia nodded. "After a few days of May, you'll be glad to see Mr. Balter again."

"No way!" Nat and James said together.

"Okay, okay." Jamal put up both hands. "But don't say we didn't warn you."

Just then the bus stopped and Eli got on. May checked her list. "Good morning, Eli," she said. "Zip up that jacket, honey. If you ask me, it's chilly today."

Nat was confused. Did Jamal count that as too friendly? May was just being nice.

A little later the bus stopped again. This time May didn't check her list. "Hello, Hank," she said. She opened her mouth to say more, but Hank didn't wait. He headed straight for the back of the bus.

Suddenly, Cody leaned into the aisle.

"Excuse me, Hank," he said politely.

Nat froze in surprise. Was Cody out of his mind? Why was he talking to Hank?

Hank stopped. He glared at Cody. "What do you want?" he snarled.

"Nothing," said Cody. "I brought these for you." He held out a sheet of colorful stickers.

Natalie recognized them at once. *The Sergeant Strong Arm stickers!* she thought. *So that's why Cody was so set on finding them. He wanted to give them to Hank.*

Hank looked at the stickers, then at Cody. His eyes narrowed in suspicion. "What's the catch? How come you're giving them to me?"

Cody shrugged. "I thought you'd like them, that's all."

Natalie held her breath. What would Hank do? Stickers were for little kids, not fifth graders—especially not fifth grade bullies.

Hank took the stickers. "Thanks," he said

gruffly. Then he went on down the aisle.

Natalie let out her breath. She didn't know who had surprised her more, Hank or her own little brother.

"I don't get it," James said to Cody. "How come you gave Hank the stickers?"

"Yeah," said Jamal. "That was a pretty gutsy move, Cody. He might have thrown them back in your face."

"Nah," said Cody. "He likes Sergeant Strong Arm. He said so yesterday."

Nat turned to look at Hank. "Hey! He's smiling," she said in surprise.

James glanced back, too. "Amazing. He looks kind of nice—like a regular kid, almost."

"Maybe I'll show him my superhero cards some day," Cody said. "I wonder which *he'd* rather be, Swamp Thing or Trash Master?"

Natalie just shook her head.

Bus Five pulled up in front of school, and kids began to get off. But it was slow going. May had something to say to everyone. What's more, she said it loud enough for the whole bus to hear.

"'Bye, Eli. See you after kindergarten. So long, Warren. Did you bring a good lunch? If you ask me, you could use some meat on your bones. 'Bye, Kate. Time for a haircut, honey. Your bangs are getting long."

Jamal grinned at Nat. "See what I mean?"

"No," she said stubbornly. But she was beginning to have second thoughts. Was May being friendly and helpful? Or was she fussing over everyone?

The line moved forward. "'Bye, Celia," said May. "Is that a flute you have there? I hope you practice a lot. Practice makes perfect, I always say."

May let Cody go with just a good-bye. But when Jamal tried to hurry past, she put out a hand to stop him. "Oh, Jamal," she said. "Do you still have that sweet little worn-out old teddy bear? I remember you

used to bring it to school every single day."

Jamal flung out his arms. "May! That was four years ago. I don't carry it around now!"

"Too bad," said May. "You looked so cute."

Jamal turned and fled from the bus.

Poor guy! thought Natalie. *How embarrassing.* Suddenly she was nervous. She was next.

"Natalie, what nice cowboy boots," May said with a smile. "You wore them yesterday, too, didn't you?"

"Yes, I did," said Nat.

"Well, if you ask me, wearing boots too often will warp your feet," said May. "What you need is a pair of sensible shoes, like mine." She pointed to her brown lace-ups.

"My boots are just fine, thank you very much," Nat said in a sharp voice. She stomped off the bus and strode toward school. James had to run to catch up with her.

"My boots do *not* warp my feet," Nat said through clenched teeth. "And even if they did, I'd never wear boring brown lace-ups. Not in a million, zillion years."

"I guess Jamal was right," said James. "May really is too friendly—"

"*And* too bossy *and* too nosy," put in Nat.

James nodded. "Now I see why the big kids try to hurry past her. They don't want to have to listen to her advice."

"And why does she keep saying 'if you ask me'?" Nat went on. "Are we supposed to ask her permission before we do something? Like, 'May I wear my boots? May I blow my nose? May I get off this stupid bus?'"

James laughed. "It sounds like that game, Mother-May-I," he said. Then he grabbed Nat's arm. "Hey! That's it. That's what we'll call May."

"Mother-May-I," Natalie said with a grin. "Of course. It's perfect."

Chapter Four

Swamp Thing or Trash Master

"I sure hope Mr. Balter's back today," Natalie said at the breakfast table Thursday morning. Then she clapped her hands to her cheeks. "I can't believe I said that. I must be nuts! I don't want Old Yeller back."

"No, but you don't want Mother-May-I, either," James said. He pushed some soggy cereal around his bowl. "How can you choose between them? It's like trying to decide if you'd rather be Swamp Thing or Trash Master."

"I'd rather be Trash Master," Cody said. "He looks yucky and he smells bad. But deep down, under all the garbage, he's a good guy. Swamp Thing's different. He creeps out of the swamp at night, and—"

"Cody! We're talking about bus drivers, not superheroes," said Natalie. She turned to James. "Between May and Mr. Balter, I guess I'd pick Mr. Balter. He's crabby and loud. But *he'd* never tell me to eat plenty of leafy green vegetables."

"Did May say that to you?" Cody asked.

"Uh-huh. Right after she reminded James to brush his teeth twice a day," said Nat.

James frowned. "She treats us like babies. He yells all the time. Let's face it. We're sunk no matter which one we get."

The three of them dawdled over breakfast, half hoping to miss the bus. But in the end they got to the stop just as Bus Five did.

May was driving.

"Here we go again," Natalie muttered. She and the others climbed on board. But today May barely seemed to notice as they hurried past her and down the aisle.

"That's weird," said James. "Mother-May-I didn't say one word to us. Not even hello."

"Hey, I'm not complaining," said Nat. "Maybe she has something on her mind—besides giving us dumb advice, I mean."

She and James took a seat in the middle of the bus. But Cody kept going till he reached the empty seats in the back.

"Cody! What are you doing?" Nat called after him. "That's where Hank sits."

"I know. I brought my trading cards to show him," Cody called back. He dug through his backpack and fished out the cards. "See? Here they are."

"Yeah, but Cody—" Nat began.

"It's okay. I'll be fine," Cody told her.

Suddenly Nat realized that the other kids on Bus Five had overheard everything. Now they were watching to see what she'd do.

"This is embarrassing," she said to James.

"Do you think I should go get him?"

"You can try," said James. "But you know Cody. Once he makes up his mind..."

"He doesn't change it. I know."

"Then why not leave him alone? Maybe he's figured out something about Hank that the rest of us missed."

"Oh, all right," said Natalie. All the same, when Hank got on the bus, she watched him closely. So did the other kids.

Hank headed for the back of the bus. But he stopped short when he saw Cody. "What are you doing here?" he said gruffly.

"Waiting for you," Cody said with a smile. "Want to see my superhero cards? I just got Crystal Gazer. She can see the future."

"Yeah, but only when the moon is full," Hank said. He sat down. Soon he and Cody were deep in conversation.

When nothing exciting happened, the other kids quickly lost interest. Natalie kept watch awhile longer. Then finally she turned

36

back around. "I guess everything's okay," she said to James.

"Sure," said James. "I bet right this minute, Cody is asking Hank if he'd rather be Swamp Thing or Trash Master."

Natalie laughed. "I bet you're right. And the funny part is, Hank probably has an answer."

A few minutes later, May parked in front of the school. She stood up and faced the kids. "Girls and boys," she said in her booming voice, "I'm sorry to say this is the last time I'll be with you on Bus Five."

Nat started to cheer. Just in time she caught herself and turned it into a cough.

James gave her an elbow in the ribs.

"It's hard to say good-bye when I'm getting to know you so well," May went on. "But my daughter just had a baby, and I've decided to go to Australia to help her out."

"She probably moved there to get away from May," James whispered.

Natalie gave *him* an elbow in the ribs.

Hannah, Anna, and Janna raised their hands. "Yes, girls?" said May.

"Who will be our driver?" asked Hannah.

"Is Mr. Balter coming back?" asked Anna.

"Or do we get someone else?" asked Janna.

"Mr. Balter is still on sick leave," said May. "Until he gets back, your driver will be Kip Hayes. He's new. I understand he used to be a sergeant in the army."

"Cool!" said Cody. "Maybe he'll be like Sergeant Strong Arm."

The other kids laughed.

"I'm sure he's a very nice man," May said. "Now, off you go, kids—and remember to stand up straight and tall. Good posture makes a good impression, I always say."

Good-bye and good riddance, I always say, Nat thought. As she walked past May, she slumped her shoulders on purpose.

James did the same. They barely made it off the bus before they burst out laughing.

Cody caught up to them. He was grinning, too. "My lucky T-shirt did it again," he said, patting his chest. "Hank promised to show me his superhero drawings tomorrow. May's going away. And Sergeant Strong Arm is going to be our bus driver."

Nat blinked in surprise. "Whoa! Back up a minute, Cody. Hank the Tank likes to draw?"

"Uh-huh. He wants to be a comic book artist when he grows up," Cody said.

"Amazing," said James. "I figured he'd want to be a football player. I mean, he's so big and strong and all."

Cody shook his head. "Hank says that's what everyone thinks. But he's not really good at sports. It's a problem because his dad is. And when Hank spends summers with him in Dallas, that's all his dad wants to do."

Natalie and James stared at Cody as if he'd just sprouted a second head. "How did you find all this out?" Natalie asked.

"Oh, I don't know. We were just talking," Cody said vaguely. "Well, 'bye, you guys. I have to go. Mr. Sato said I could be the kindergarten line leader today." He started for the door.

Natalie suddenly felt proud of her little brother. "You were right, James," she said softly. "Cody *did* find out stuff about Hank that the rest of us missed."

"Really," said James. "But I want to know one more thing." He cupped his hands around his mouth. "Hey, Cody!" he called. "Which would Hank rather be, Swamp Thing or Trash Master?"

"Trash Master, of course!" Cody called back. "Same as me."

Chapter Five

Sergeant Strong Arm

Brrrrring! The bell rang at the end of the school day. Natalie and James joined the other kids scrambling for jackets and backpacks in the coat room.

"'Bye, everyone," Ms. Donovan said over the noise. "Remember, we'll be discussing the Fun Fair tomorrow morning. So please come prepared. I can't wait to hear all your terrific ideas for new games and activities."

James and Nat headed for the bus. "So what's *your* terrific idea?" he asked her.

"I don't have one yet," said Natalie. "How about you?"

James shook his head. "I haven't even thought about the fair since Monday. I've had bus drivers on the brain."

"Me, too," said Nat. "First Mr. Balter, then May, and now Kip Hayes. I've been wondering all day what he'll be like."

"I think we're about to find out," said James.

A tall man was standing next to Bus Five. He had on dark pants and a white knit shirt. He had very short hair and very big muscles.

"Wow! If that's Mr. Hayes, he really is Sergeant Strong Arm," said Nat.

They joined the crowd of kids waiting to board the bus.

"Atten-*tion!*" said the tall man. "I want to see a line here. A *straight* line. Show me a squad I can be proud of."

He didn't shout, and he didn't sound mean. But he made it clear that he was the boss. The kids fell all over one another trying to do as he said.

The man paced the line. "Not too bad... but you can do better," he said with a tight smile. "Now listen up, all of you. My name is Kip Hayes. You will call me Mr. Hayes or sir. You will get on the bus quickly and sit down immediately. Then you will be quiet. If that is clear, say, 'Yes, sir.'"

"Yes, sir," the kids said.

Mr. Hayes cupped an ear with his hand. "I didn't hear you."

"YES, SIR!" the kids shouted.

"Good. I can see we're going to get along just fine," said Mr. Hayes. "Now march."

The kids marched. They didn't push each other getting on the bus. They didn't argue or tease. In fact, they hardly talked at all. In record time, everyone was sitting quietly and Bus Five was on its way.

Natalie looked around, amazed. "What do you think?" she whispered to James.

"About Mr. Hayes? Well, he seems pretty strict. But he doesn't yell, and he doesn't treat us like babies. So that's good," James whispered back. Then he looked puzzled. "Why are we whispering?"

"Because the bus is so quiet. That's what I was asking you about, not Mr. Hayes," said Nat. "Don't you think it's a little weird?"

James shrugged. "Not really. Anyway, it won't last. By tomorrow we'll be used to Mr. Hayes. Then everything will be back to normal."

"I guess you're right," said Natalie.

Bus Five dropped them off at the Adamses' house as usual. Mrs. Adams was in the backyard with Cody and three of his friends—Eli, David L., and David E.

"Hi, kids!" she called. "We've got a hot game of soccer going here. Want to play?"

"Thanks," said James, "but we need to think up an idea for the Fun Fair."

"Plus we have lots of writing practice." Nat rolled her eyes.

"Okay," said her mom. "There's apple

juice in the fridge and a bowl of popcorn on the kitchen table. Help yourselves."

Nat and James went to the kitchen. They each got a glass of juice. Then they sat down with the bowl of popcorn between them and talked about the fair. Twenty minutes later, the bowl was half empty. But they hadn't come up with any terrific new ideas.

Suddenly, David E. came running into the kitchen. "Bathroom...quick!" he panted.

"Down the hall on the left," Natalie said.

David E. disappeared down the hall. A moment later, Cody came in to get a tissue. He stayed to grab a handful of popcorn. Then he and David E. went back outside. No sooner had they left than Eli came in for a drink. Then David L. passed through the kitchen on his way to the bathroom. And David E. and Cody both came back in for popcorn.

"What is this, a parade?" said Nat. "Make

up your minds, you guys. In or out."

"A parade," James repeated. "That's it, Nat! We can have a parade for the Fun Fair."

Nat looked puzzled. "You mean a costume parade like the one we have at Halloween?"

"No, I mean a pet parade," said James. "Kids could bring their pets and walk them around the schoolyard. It would be a great way to start the fair."

Natalie didn't say anything. She could tell that James really loved this idea. His eyes were shining, the way they always did when he talked about animals. He also had two cats, a dog, and plenty of other pets to enter in the parade. But she and Cody didn't even have a gerbil. They would be left out.

"A pet parade," repeated Eli. "Cool! I could bring my dog."

"And I could bring my guinea pig," said David E. "I'd put his cage in my wagon."

"What about me and Nat?" Cody said.

"We don't have any pets. Dad's allergic."

"Nat's not going to be in the parade, and neither am I," said James. "If the PTA likes the idea, we're going to be judges. We'll give out prizes for the best pets in the parade. You can be our helper, Cody."

Suddenly, Nat felt a lot better. She and Cody both smiled.

Mrs. Adams came into the kitchen. "May I join the party? Or do I have to stay outside with the soccer ball?" she teased.

"Oops! Sorry, Mom," said Cody.

"That's okay." She took a handful of popcorn. "What are we celebrating, anyway?"

"The great idea James had for the fair," Nat said. "We're going to have a pet parade."

"Sounds like fun," said her mom.

"I have a great idea, too," put in Cody.

"What is it?" asked James.

Cody's chin went up. "I can't tell you yet," he said.

"Well, you'd better tell somebody by Monday," Nat said. "That's when the ideas are due."

"I know," Cody said. "I'll be ready. I just have to ask someone a favor first."

The next morning it was raining hard. Natalie and James stood at the bus stop, trying to stay dry in their slickers and hoods. But Cody went looking for puddles.

Splat! splat! splat! He stamped through the water. Then he hit a really deep puddle. *Splash!* Water sprayed all over his legs.

"Oh, no! My pants are wet!" he yelled.

"Gee, what a surprise," said Nat. "It's only water, Cody. It'll dry soon enough."

"Forget it. I'm going back to the house to change," said Cody.

James grabbed Cody's arm. "Wait! The bus will be here any minute. You don't want to miss Sergeant Strong Arm, do you?"

Cody tried to pull free. "I don't care," he said. "He isn't the real Sergeant Strong Arm, and I don't like him one little bit."

"Then what about Hank?" Nat said quickly. "Isn't he going to show you his drawings today? You don't want to miss that."

"Oh, yeah. I forgot," Cody said.

He stopped struggling, and James let go of him. A minute later Bus Five arrived and the three kids got on board.

Mr. Hayes stopped them at the top of the steps. "Hold it right there," he said. "Starting today, we're filling the bus from the back to the front. Everyone has an assigned seat."

He checked a seating chart attached to a clipboard. "Penny, James. Adams, Natalie. You will sit in the second seat on your right. Adams, Cody. You will sit in the second seat on your left. These are your permanent seats. Remember them. That is all."

James frowned. "Why do we have to—"

"That is all," Mr. Hayes repeated in an icy tone. "Sit down, Penny, and be quiet."

"My name is James," James muttered. But he sat down promptly, and so did the others.

Natalie looked around. No one on Bus Five was talking or laughing. No one was even smiling. In fact, Hannah, Anna, and Janna looked as if they might cry. Usually they squeezed into one seat together. But Mr. Hayes's seating chart had separated them.

"Boy, was I wrong," whispered James. "Everything's *not* back to normal today."

"So I noticed," said Nat. "I feel as if we've all been sent to the principal's office—only we haven't done anything wrong."

When Eli got on the bus, Mr. Hayes told him to sit next to Cody. A little later Hank climbed on board, and Mr. Hayes gave him the seat in front of Cody.

Cody's face lit up. "Hi, Hank," he said.

Nat nudged James. "At least *someone's* happy about the new seats," she murmured.

Hank took a folder from his backpack and handed it to Cody. "Here are the drawings I told you about," he said softly.

Cody opened the folder eagerly and started looking through the drawings. "Wow! These are great, Hank. Look, Eli. Look how neat. Here's Captain Courage...and Sergeant Strong Arm...and Crystal Gazer."

"Cool!" said Eli. "Pass me some more."

Natalie was curious. What was all the fuss about? She leaned across the aisle to see—and her eyes widened in surprise. Hank's drawings were done in pencil on lined notebook paper. But otherwise, they looked just like the comics.

"Hank! You're really good!" she burst out. Her words seemed to echo through the quiet bus. Everyone stared at her.

"I mean it, Hank," she said in a softer voice. "You're a real artist."

"Thanks," said Hank. Then he blushed bright red.

Chapter Six

The Wild Man

"Let's take a vote," Ms. Donovan said. "Is everyone ready?"

Natalie, James, and the other kids in the class nodded. They'd spent the first part of the morning talking about the school fair. Ms. Donovan had listed their ideas on the chalkboard in her beautiful, looping cursive. Now it was time to make the final choice.

"Think about all the ideas," Ms. Donovan said. "Then write your vote—in cursive—on a piece of paper."

Natalie almost laughed. Somehow, her teacher turned everything into writing practice. She got out a piece of paper and carefully wrote down her vote: *Pet parade!*

While Ms. Donovan counted the votes, Nat crossed her fingers for good luck. *Please, please let it be the pet parade*, she wished.

Finally, Ms. Donovan looked up. "The winner is...the pet parade," she said.

The kids cheered, James and Natalie the loudest of all.

"Congratulations, James," Ms. Donovan said. "You can write a proposal—that's a description of your idea—this weekend. We'll turn it in to the PTA on Monday."

"Can Natalie help me?" James said quickly. "It was kind of her idea, too."

"Sure," said Ms. Donovan. "And may I offer a suggestion? Make sure you have lots of prize categories. I mean something besides biggest, smallest, youngest, and oldest pets. That way, more kids can win."

James thought for a moment. "How about longest ears and shortest tail?" he said.

"Good," said Ms. Donovan. "What else?"

The class started calling out ideas.

"Most spots."

"Best dressed."

"Most unusual."

"Scariest."

"Softest."

"Excellent," said Ms. Donovan. She turned to Nat and James. "How about writing these down?"

"In cursive?" Natalie squeaked.

Ms. Donovan laughed. "It's okay, Natalie. You may print...this time."

"Whew!" said Natalie. "That's a relief!"

Over the weekend, she and James worked on their proposal. Cody worked on his idea, too. But he wanted to keep it a surprise. So he dictated it to his dad— behind closed doors.

On Monday the kids turned in their proposals. Then they had to wait. The PTA was meeting Wednesday evening to decide on activities for the fair. The final choices would be posted on the main bulletin board Thursday morning.

In the meantime, school went on as usual, and Mr. Hayes continued to drive Bus Five.

"Do you think Mr. Balter's ever coming back?" Natalie said at lunch on Wednesday.

"I sure hope so," said Warren. "I really hate being called Smiley all the time."

"Tell me about it," said James. "All I hear is, 'Line up, Penny. Sit down, Penny. Be quiet, Penny.'"

"The bus is already too quiet," said Nat. "I think it's creepy. We're like a bunch of zombies in a graveyard."

"At least you and James get to sit together up front," said Kate. "I'm stuck in the last row, and I get carsick every time."

"Kate, that's terrible!" said Nat.

"Maybe Mr. Hayes would let you change seats," said James. "Have you asked him?"

"No," Kate said miserably. "I'm too scared." She looked from James to Natalie. "Could you guys talk to him for me?"

"Yeah, could you?" said Warren. "After all, you got Hank to stop being a bully. So maybe you could get Mr. Hayes to change his rules—for everyone."

"We could try," said Natalie.

"*We?*" said James. Then he sighed. "Oh, all right. But *we* aren't promising anything. Okay?"

"Okay," said Kate. "Thanks, you guys."

At ten minutes to three that afternoon, Nat and James left the school building. They had explained their errand to Ms. Donovan, and she'd let them go early. Now they were on their way to talk to Mr. Hayes.

Bus Five was parked at the curb. But Mr. Hayes wasn't behind the wheel. He was on the grass nearby—doing push-ups with one arm. His muscles bulged. He looked very tough.

Natalie's mouth went dry. She licked her lips nervously. "Maybe this wasn't such a great idea," she said to James.

"Not one of your better ones," he agreed. "But it's too late to turn back now."

Mr. Hayes bounced to his feet. He wasn't even breathing hard. "Penny. Adams. You're early," he said sternly.

"Uh—yes, I guess we are," said James.

"There's something we'd like to talk to you about," Nat said in a rush.

"Okay. You can do it while I finish my workout," said Mr. Hayes. "I've got to exercise every chance I get. Driving a bus is bad for my muscle tone." He lay down on the grass and started doing sit-ups. "Good thing today's my last day to substitute."

"What?" said James.

"Mr. Balter's coming back?" said Natalie.

"No, he decided to retire," said Mr. Hayes. "Some new guy's taken the job."

Just then the dismissal bell rang. Mr.

Hayes stood up. "What was it you wanted to talk to me about?" he asked.

Nat and James grinned at each other.

"Oh, nothing important," said Nat.

"It doesn't matter now," said James.

"Then get moving," said Mr. Hayes. "I want to see a line here. A *straight* line."

When the rest of the Bus Five kids arrived, Nat and James told them the news.

"No more Mr. Hayes?" said Hannah.

"No more assigned seats?" said Anna.

"We'll be together again!" said Janna.

The three of them jumped up and down and hugged each other. Kate and Warren acted as if Nat and James had somehow arranged the whole thing just for them.

The other kids were happy, too. They still made a straight line to get on the bus. They still sat in their assigned seats. But they were not quiet on the ride home—no matter what Mr. Hayes said.

The next morning Natalie was up early.

She put on her favorite western shirt and her softest jeans. Then she added her belt with the horseshoe-shaped buckle. Horseshoes were lucky, and she could use some luck today.

Nat hurried down the hall to her brother's room. Cody was still fast asleep. She opened the curtains to let in the sunlight. "Wake up, sleepyhead," she called sweetly.

Cody sat up. "Huh? What?" He covered his eyes. "Ahhhgh! Close the curtains, Nat! My eyeballs are frying."

"Okay, okay." Nat closed the curtains. "I just wanted to ask you to wear your lucky T-shirt today."

Cody gave her a suspicious look. "How come? You hate that shirt."

"True. But we're getting a new bus driver today. And we're going to find out which activities the PTA chose for the fair." Nat shrugged. "We need all the luck we can get. Maybe your shirt will help."

"Okay," said Cody. "But you have to promise not to make fun of it ever again."

Nat sighed. "I promise."

"Good," said Cody. "Now go away. I'm going back to sleep."

Natalie went down to the kitchen. She had part of her breakfast with her parents and the rest when James arrived. Cody got up so late, he had only fifteen minutes to eat. But he did remember to wear his lucky shirt under his regular T-shirt.

As the kids waited at the bus stop, Nat's stomach began to feel fluttery. *What will the new driver be like?* she wondered. After the two strange substitutes, it was hard to know what to expect.

Bus Five rounded the bend in the road. Nat shaded her eyes, trying to see the man behind the wheel. There was something odd about the shape of his head.

The bus pulled over and the doors opened. The driver was wearing a hat with cloth moose antlers! He also had on a polka-dot shirt and checkered high-top sneakers.

Nat and James stepped back in surprise. Cody's sleepy eyes popped wide open.

"*Bonjour.* I am zee new host for Bus Five," the driver said in a fake French accent. "Zhere are sree in your party? Please to come in. I am sure we can find you some lovely seats. Do you prefer zee window or zee aisle? Zee right side or zee left?"

Is this guy for real? thought Natalie. *He talks like a cartoon character, and he looks like a clown!* She hesitated, not sure she wanted to board the bus. But Cody went right ahead, so she and James had to follow.

"I like your hat," Cody told the driver.

"You have excellent taste," the driver replied in a regular voice. "What is your name, O young but intelligent one?"

"Cody Adams," said Cody. "This is my big sister, Natalie, and this is James Penny." He pointed to Nat and James in turn.

"I'm Richard DeVries," the driver said. "You can call me Richard, or you can call me Rick. But you can't call me Rich because I don't have much money." He gave the kids a toothy grin. "Now find a seat, one and all. It's time to blast off."

Natalie, James, and Cody sat down.

"Bus Five to ground control. We're ready for countdown," said Rick. "Ten, nine, eight, seven, six, five, four, three, two, one—" He made a sound like a rocket blasting off. Then he pulled into the road.

Natalie grabbed the arm of her seat and held on for dear life. Rick DeVries was a wild man! There was no telling what might happen with him at the wheel.

Chapter Seven

The Fall Fun Fair

Bus Five didn't take off like a rocket. Rick drove at regular speeds. He signaled his turns and obeyed the traffic signs. He didn't even say anything weird when he picked up Eli and Hank.

Maybe I was wrong, thought Natalie. *Maybe he isn't so crazy after all.*

She was just beginning to relax when Rick called out, "Okay, campers. It's sing-along time. I'm sure you know this little tune." Then he started to sing in a big, dramatic voice, "*In diesen heiligen Hallen...*"

The kids all stared at him.

"Is he nuts?" James exclaimed. "That

sounds like some opera he's singing!"

Nat heaved a big sigh. "Why can't we have a nice, normal driver for once? This guy's worse than the last three put together."

Rick broke into laughter. "Just joking," he said. "Let's try again." Then he sang, "The wheels on the bus go round and round, round and round, round and round...."

Right away, the younger kids joined in. They finished that verse. Then Rick began another. "The driver on the bus is a way cool dude, way cool dude, way cool dude...."

James rolled his eyes. "Yup, he's nuts all right."

"No question about it," Nat said over the noise. "But give him credit for one thing. At least we're not zombies anymore."

Bus Five pulled up in front of the school. Nat and James started for the door. But Cody was holding up the line. He'd stopped to talk to Rick.

"Excuse me," Cody said. "Are you a real bus driver—or just a pretend one?"

"Both," said Rick. "Driving a bus is my job. But I'm really an artist."

"Hey, so's my friend Hank!" said Cody. He pulled Hank forward by the arm. "His drawings are the best. You should see them!"

Rick smiled. "I'd like that," he said.

Hank's eyes lit up. "You really mean it?"

"Sure," said Rick. "Anytime."

The kids went on into school. Cody, Nat, and James joined the crowd studying the PTA bulletin board in the front hall.

"I see it!" James shouted. "There it is!"

Nat looked where he was pointing. Sure enough, their proposal had been posted on the board. It had been chosen for the fair!

"All right! We did it!" she yelled. She and James gave each other high fives.

"Look! Mine's there, too," said Cody. He pointed to a page titled "Superhero Beanbag Toss." Next to it was a pencil drawing on notebook paper. It showed Captain Courage and Sergeant Strong Arm, with circles where their stomachs, hands, and knees would be.

"Did Hank do the drawing?" asked James.

"Uh-huh. That's the favor I told you about," said Cody. "The idea is, we paint the superheroes on boards and cut holes where the circles are. Then at the fair, kids toss beanbags through the holes to win prizes."

"Neat," said James.

"It's a great idea," said Nat.

"Wow! Both our ideas got picked for the fair. That's really lucky," said Cody. He lifted his shirt, grinning broadly. "Here, Nat. You can say thank you to my T-shirt."

Natalie laughed. "No way," she said. "I promised I wouldn't make fun of it. I didn't say I'd talk to it."

James grabbed her arm. "Come on, Nat. Let's go to class. I bet everyone will be psyched about the pet parade."

As it turned out, the parade was popular with the whole school. By the time Nat and James boarded the bus at the end of the day, everyone was talking about it.

"Hey, Nat," said Jamal. "Can a parrot be in the parade?"

"Sure," said Natalie.

"How about a mouse?" asked Dylan.

"How about a moose?" asked Rick. He tipped his antler hat.

"Yes to the mouse. No to the moose—unless it's the four-footed kind," said James.

"Rats!" said Rick. "Or should I say, 'Mice'?" He grinned into the rear-view mirror. "Say, that reminds me of a riddle. Natalie, why is a mouse like grass?"

"I don't know," said Natalie. "Why?"

"Because the cattle eat it," said Rick. "Get it? Cat'll—cat will eat it."

Nat and the other kids groaned.

Rick grinned. "Better be nice to me, or I'll start singing," he said. Then he burst into song. "Oh, I went to the animal fair. The mouses and mooses were there...."

James and Natalie just shook their heads. The wild man was at it again.

He was at it again the next day and the school days that followed. He sang songs and made up rhymes and told jokes. He pretended the bus was a train or a plane or a submarine. He pointed out things that appealed to him as an artist—sun streaming through the trees, an old weathered bridge.

Nat and James couldn't figure Rick out. They never knew what he'd do next. But they were too busy getting ready for the fair to worry much about him.

Finally, the big day arrived. Natalie, James, and their families got to the school early to help set up.

"Come and see my game," Cody said eagerly. He led the others past the food stands and the craft tables to the games area. Hank was already there. He was helping Cody's teacher, Mr. Sato, set up the beanbag boards.

"Look!" said Cody. "Hank painted the superheroes. Aren't they great?"

Captain Courage and Sergeant Strong Arm were painted life-size in bright colors against a white background.

"Wow!" said Natalie. "You did a fantastic job, Hank."

"Thanks," said Hank. "But I couldn't have done it without Rick."

"You mean our bus driver?" said James.

Hank nodded. "I'd never worked with paints before—only pencil. So I asked him to show me how. He was really nice about it, and he taught me a lot. He even invited me to come to his studio to paint."

Natalie blinked in surprise. Hank seemed so happy. It was hard to believe he was the same boy who used to bully the kids on Bus Five. And what about Rick? Who could have guessed that he'd be so helpful and nice?

When Cody's idea had been accepted, he'd decided not to help with the parade. He wanted to work the beanbag game with Hank and Mr. Sato instead. So James and Natalie went to the parade meeting place on their own.

"I've been thinking," Natalie said. slowly. "Remember how we liked May and Mr. Hayes at first—and how they turned out to be yucky? Well, it's the opposite with Rick. He's turning out to be better than we thought."

"You're right," said James. "Maybe he's a wild man. But underneath all the crazy stuff, he's a pretty good guy." He grinned. "Kind of like Trash Master."

Natalie laughed. "It just goes to show— you can't judge a man by his moose hat." Then she and James had to stop talking because kids were arriving with their pets.

Jamal came with his parrot on his shoulder. Dylan had his mouse in his shirt pocket. There were dogs in all sizes and cats in all colors. There were rabbits and hamsters, gerbils and guinea pigs. There was also a lot of noise.

People talked, dogs barked, cats meowed, and the parrot squawked. It said, "I t'ought I taw a puddy tat," over and over, till Nat thought she'd go nuts. Luckily, the kids from Ms. Donovan's class got things under control, and the judging could begin.

There were first, second, and third prize ribbons. Nat and James gave the Biggest Pet award to a St. Bernard named Ox. They gave the Smallest Pet award to a cricket in a bamboo cage. Scariest went to a tarantula. Fluffiest went to Celia's Persian cat. And Best Dressed went to Hannah's rabbit. It was wearing doll clothes and riding in a stroller. Jamal's parrot got Biggest Mouth.

Everyone who didn't get a ribbon got a fancy certificate. Ms. Donovan had made them up on the computer. The only

problem was, each one had to be signed.

"Very sneaky," said Nat. "More cursive!" She was signing what seemed to be the ninety-ninth certificate when she heard a lot of laughter. She looked up. There was Rick.

He was wearing his moose antler hat. He also had on a fuzzy brown costume with black felt hooves over his hands and feet.

Natalie cracked up. Rick looked so funny—like a cartoon moose with a human face.

"Hi, there," he said. "I heard that only four-footed moose could be in the parade. So I came prepared." He waved his front hooves.

James grinned at Natalie. "What do you think? Should we let him be in the parade?"

"Be in it?" said Nat. "I think he should *lead* it!" She took one of Rick's hooves and James took the other. Then they marched around the school, with all the kids and pets behind them.